MEET THE AUTHOR - WES MAGEE

What is your favourite animal?
A cat called Rusty
What is your favourite boy's name?
Kingsley
What is your favourite girl's name?
Miranda
What is your favourite food?
Spaghetti
What is your favourite music?
Reggae (especially UB40)
What is your favourite hobby?
Building waterfalls in
Thorgill Beck

MEET THE ILLUSTRATOR - ANTHONY LEWIS

What is your favourite animal?
Cats
What is your favourite boy's name?
Stephen
What is your favourite girl's name?
Victoria
What is your favourite food?
Yorkshire pudding
What is your favourite music?
Blur and Lyle Lovett
What is your favourite hobby?
Going to the theatre and travel

For John Cotton

Contents

1   The Blizzard   1

2   The Animals   11

3   WinterWorld   23

4   The Gathering   33

5   The HotSpotters   43

6   War   51

7   Now What?   61

8   Who Won the War?   69

Chapter 1
The Blizzard

"Polar!" shouted Abbi. "Stop that!"

The furry, white puppy was scratching at the farmhouse door.

Abbi picked up the pet she'd been given as a Christmas present three days before. "You're just like a little polar bear," she said and hugged the wriggling puppy.

"Justin, I'm going to take Polar out for a run. Will you and Rory come with me?"

Justin was Abbi's older brother. He and their cousin Rory were sitting with their feet up against the kitchen stove. They were looking at computer magazines.

"It's snowing out there," Justin told her.

"But Polar wants a run," said Abbi. "I know we told Mum and Dad that we'd stay in until they got back from their shopping trip, but Polar wants to go out *now*. Please come with me, Justin, *please*."

"OK, Abbi, OK," said Justin. He knew his sister was so crazy about animals that she'd keep on and on until he agreed. He stood up and said, "Just a quick run, right? And only around the farmyard, Abbi. You can't go up on the moor in this weather."

Abbi smiled. "Keep still, Polar," she said as she put a collar and lead on the excited puppy.

Justin, Rory and Abbi pulled on their coats, boots and gloves, and stepped outside into the yard at High Farm. They walked into a wintry world. Snow was falling from a grey sky. It was mid-afternoon but already the light was fading. Beyond the farmyard a chill wind whistled across the snowy moor.

"Remember," warned Justin, "we stay in the farmyard, right?"

"Right," said Abbi.

Rory wiped the snowflakes from his glasses.

He was the same age as Abbi, and was staying with his cousins for the Christmas

holidays. He was a city boy, smaller and skinnier than Justin, and he wasn't used to snowy weather like this. He shivered in the cold wind, and huddled into his coat to keep warm.

Justin and Abbi looked at him and shrugged their shoulders.

"Polar, stop pulling!" ordered Abbi as the energetic puppy jumped and snapped at snowflakes.

"Polar, behave!" Abbi said and gave the lead a sharp tug. It parted from the collar and the puppy was free. He bounded away across the snowy farmyard.

"Polar!" shouted Abbi. "Come here!"

The furry, white puppy ignored her. He raced out of the farmyard and onto the open moor. In seconds he had vanished into the swirling snow.

"Polar!" shouted Abbi. "Polar!" She ran to the farmyard gate.

"Leave him," said Justin.

"He'll come back," said Rory.

But Polar didn't come back. Abbi, Justin and Rory stood at the gate as the snow swirled faster. Now the wind was howling across the moor.

"Polar!" shouted Abbi.

Justin pointed a gloved finger at his animal-crazy sister. "It was *you* who let him go, Abbi," he said crossly.

"I couldn't help it," protested Abbi. "Polar just broke away ..."

"... and now he's gone," said Rory. "We'll never find him in this – this blizzard."

Abbi felt frantic. "I've got to find him," she said, and she ran onto the moor. Like her puppy, she quickly vanished in the swirling snow.

"Abbi, come back here!" shouted Justin, but his voice was lost in the howling wind.

"Now what do we do?" asked Rory.

"We'll have to find them," said Justin.

"But it's blowing a blizzard," protested Rory.

"I know that," said Justin, "but we can't leave Abbi and that mad puppy out there in this weather, right? They could die! We've no choice, we've got to find them, Rory. Come on!"

The boys set off across the moor. They bent into the driving wind and battled through the blizzard. Within a minute they looked like walking snowmen.

"Abbi! Polar!" shouted Justin. "Where are you?" The only reply came from the wind. It howled like an animal in pain.

The blizzard grew worse. Rory could see nothing through his snow-covered glasses. He grabbed hold of Justin's coat.

"Rory," shouted Justin. "Hold tight. We must stay together."

The boys struggled to keep going but there was no sight of Abbi or Polar. They felt as if they were being lifted off their feet by the strong wind.

"What's happening?" cried Rory.

"I don't know," shouted Justin, "but I feel as if we're being swept away, Rory. Hang on!"

A sudden, great blast of wind threw the boys up into the freezing air. They were blinded by snowflakes, and could hardly breathe, as they were hurled high into the darkening sky. Up, and up, and up they went.

As helpless as two dead leaves, the boys twisted and turned with the force of the blizzard. The wind's howl filled their ears as Justin and Rory were swept up and away ...

Up and away.

Chapter 2
The Animals

Justin and Rory were spun round and round at the centre of the blizzard. They felt as if they were being torn apart.

"Hang on, Rory!" shouted Justin.

It seemed a long time before the blizzard calmed down and the boys tumbled to earth. Landing like sky-divers, they rolled forward before ending up in a snowdrift. They scrambled up, spitting snow.

"Where are we?" wailed Rory.

Justin looked around and was amazed by what he saw. They were standing in the middle of a snowfield. The blizzard had passed, the wind had gone, and all around there was stillness and silence.

Overhead, Justin saw a pink sky. No clouds. No sun. Just smooth pinkness. Below the snowfield, a frozen lake stretched away to left and right. The ice looked thick, and was green. A dark pine forest ran along the side of the lake.

"Where are we?" Rory said again. "And why's the sky that funny colour, and why's the ice green?"

"We're no longer on the moor," said Justin. He looked worried. "And we're nowhere near High Farm."

"Look over there," said Rory, pointing.

Justin looked across the frozen lake and saw mountains over on the far side – mountains that were covered in snow.

"This is really weird," said Justin. "I've never seen a place like this before. It's as if we've ..."

"... fallen through a black hole," said Rory.

Justin looked at Rory.

"You know, like one of those black holes in space," said Rory, "where you fall into a different part of the universe. Somehow or other that blizzard's blown us into ... another world."

Justin felt worried. "Look, Rory," he said, "if we are in another world, then where are we? I mean, what sort of world is it? And how, Rory, do we get back home?"

Rory pressed his glasses down onto his nose. "I don't know, Justin," he said.

A shout made the boys turn quickly. There, not far off on the snowfield, was Abbi. She was waving madly.

"Abbi!" called Justin. "You're safe!"

She stumbled towards the two boys, shaking snow from her long hair.

"Where's Polar?" asked Justin.

"No idea," said Abbi. "He's still lost."

They called and whistled, but there was no sign of the puppy.

"He's gone," said Justin. "Sorry, Abbi, but it is just one of those things."

Abbi looked miserable.

"What's important now," said Justin, "is to find a way out of this place and to get back home, right?"

"But which way do we go?" asked Rory. "Which way? This way? That way?"

No-one knew. They were trying to decide when Abbi saw something coming out of the pine forest. "Look," she said, pointing in surprise. "A deer!"

"That's a *rein*deer, Abbi," Rory corrected her. "Like the ones they have in Lapland."

"Is that where we are?" asked Abbi. "Lapland?"

"No way," said Rory. "They don't have a pink sky or green ice there."

The children saw more reindeer coming out of the forest. The animals stood at the edge of the frozen lake, and then one by one, they stepped onto the green ice and headed away towards the far-off mountains.

Abbi was excited. "Reindeer! How fantastic!" she said. She gazed in surprise as more and more animals came out from under the dark pine trees.

First came white Arctic foxes, then a huge moose and some lolloping, white Arctic hares. After that a pack of wolves trotted across. All the animals followed the reindeer across the frozen lake.

"It's odd," said Rory. "They are all animals from cold climates."

"Odd too," said Justin, "that the wolves aren't chasing the deer or the hares."

"Aren't they fantastic!" said Abbi, loudly. Her eyes glowed.

Justin felt afraid. "Keep quiet, Abbi," he warned. "They're wild animals, not pets. They could attack us."

But Abbi was too excited to be silent. "Justin! Rory! Look!" she cried. "A polar bear!"

They watched as a large polar bear lumbered to the edge of the lake.

"What's that behind it?" asked Rory.

Abbi's eyes almost popped out of her head. "It's – it's Polar! It's my puppy!" she cried.

The large, white bear stepped onto the green ice and headed after the other animals. Polar went too. He slipped and skidded along behind the polar bear.

"Polar!" called Abbi, but her furry, white puppy just kept on going. "Why's he following all those animals?" asked Abbi. "And why won't he come when I call?"

Justin was puzzled. He stared at the long line of animals making their way across the frozen lake.

"Where's Polar going?" said Abbi. She was almost in tears.

"He's going with those animals," said Justin, "and they're all heading for the mountains on the far side of the lake.

"But why?" asked Abbi.

"I don't know," said Justin. He shook his head. "I just don't know."

"But maybe *he* does," said Rory. He pointed to the pine forest.

Justin, Abbi and Rory saw a creature walk out of the forest's darkness. It was covered in furs from head to foot, but it wasn't an animal.

It was a man.

Chapter 3
WinterWorld

The man looked big in his layers of furs. His face was deeply lined and he had a tangled beard. He saw the three children and pointed at them with a sharp stick.

Justin, Abbi and Rory froze.

"Hey! You three!" called the Fur Man. "Come here!"

As if they were walking in their sleep, the children plodded across the snowfield towards him. At the edge of the frozen lake they stopped in front of the Fur Man. He walked slowly around them. "Who are you?" he asked.

The children felt too scared to reply.

The Fur Man frowned. "*Who are you*?" he repeated. "Have the HotSpotters sent you?"

"The hot what?" asked Rory.

The Fur Man frowned again.

Justin spoke out. "We're lost," he said. "We were blown away in a blizzard, and now we don't know where we are ..."

"Oh, you must be from WarmWorld," said the Fur Man, and his frown turned into a smile. "The HotSpotters haven't sent you. You're WarmWorlders."

He held out a fur-gloved hand to Justin. "Welcome to WinterWorld," he said. "My name's Freeza."

Justin shook hands, feeling confused.

Freeza shouted, and twenty or more Fur People came out of the pine forest. There were men, women and children, and all were well wrapped up in furs. Like Freeza, they carried sticks. They looked scared when they saw Justin, Abbi and Rory.

"Don't worry," Freeza told them. "They're from WarmWorld." He laughed, and the Fur People smiled.

Justin could keep quiet no longer. "Look," he said, "I've got some questions, and I want some answers, please."

The Fur People looked at him.

"You said we're in WinterWorld, right?" said Justin. "But where's that? And who are you? And what's going on here?"

The Fur People shuffled their fur-wrapped feet.

"And I've lost my puppy," Abbi told them. "He's called Polar, and he's gone across the lake with those other animals, and he won't come back when I call, and he's ..." she ran out of words. All she could do was point across the frozen lake.

Freeza spoke to the children.

"You're in WinterWorld," he said, "and we're the Fur People. We live here. This is our home. We're all WinterWorlders. You three are from WarmWorld. You have the sun. There's no sun here in WinterWorld. It's winter all the time."

"I was right," said Rory. "We *did* fall through a black hole."

But Justin wanted to know more. "What about all the animals?" he asked. "Where are they going?" He looked at Freeza. "There's something strange happening here, isn't there?"

Freeza looked across the frozen lake towards the far-off mountains. "You're right," he said. "All the animals and Fur People of WinterWorld have been called to the Gathering."

"The Gathering?" asked Justin. "What's that?"

"It's a special meeting," Freeza told him. "You see, animals and Fur People live together in peace in WinterWorld, but now there is a great danger facing us all. Our Winter Queen has called the Gathering to tell us all about it. To tell us about this terrible danger."

The Fur People groaned. They looked scared.

"What is this terrible danger?" asked Justin.

"Sorry," said Freeza, and he waved his stick, "but there's no time to tell you now. We must move on, or we'll be late for the Gathering."

Freeza looked at Justin, Abbi and Rory. "Why don't you three come with us? We're going to need all the help we can get."

The three children stood in the snow and watched the Fur People go.

"Now what do we do?" asked Abbi. "We're lost in a strange world – and Polar's gone – and ..." She was close to tears.

"And we don't know how to get home," said Justin.

"Then there's only one thing we can do," said Rory.

"What's that?" asked Justin and Abbi.

Rory pressed his glasses down onto his nose. "We'll have to go with the Fur People and animals," he said. "If we go to the Gathering we might find someone there who can show us how to get home. It's our only chance."

Justin felt worried, but he said, "I guess you're right, Rory."

"And I'll find Polar," said Abbi, and the smile was back on her face.

The children began their journey across the frozen lake. At first they slipped and fell on the green ice, picked themselves up, and then slipped and fell again.

"We should shuffle and slide like the Fur People," said Rory. "That's the easy way to move on the ice – shuffle and slide."

Abbi and Justin looked at their cousin. He seemed to know all the answers.

They soon learnt the trick of sliding across the green ice and began to catch up with the Fur People and animals. Abbi and Rory enjoyed the thrill of sliding, but Justin was still worried. Questions buzzed in his head. *Would they ever get back home?*

Were his parents back from their shopping trip yet? What would they do when they found the children had vanished from High Farm? What was the Gathering all about? And what was the terrible danger that was facing WinterWorld?

A shout from Abbi broke into the boy's thoughts. "Justin! Rory! Look!" she shouted and pointed to a gap between the mountains. Something was shining like silver. "What is it?" asked Abbi.

"It's a glacier," said Rory. "It's a massive wall of ice between two mountains."

"And that's where the animals and the Fur People are going," said Abbi excitedly. "They're all heading towards the glacier."

Chapter 4
The Gathering

By the time Justin, Abbi and Rory reached the glacier, the animals and the Fur People had vanished inside. "They must have gone in through that split in the ice wall," said Justin.

The split was wide, and three Fur Men were on guard there.

"Stop!" ordered the biggest Fur Man, and he held up his stick. "Who are you?"

"We're from WarmWorld," said Justin. "Freeza invited us to the Gathering."

"OK, pass," said the Fur Man. "But get a move on. The Gathering's starting soon."

The children went inside the glacier and began moving along a winding passage of ice. They slid along the ice floor, and moved faster and faster as they went deeper and deeper into the glacier.

"Look at the colours," said Abbi, as green and blue light danced on the passage walls.

"The light is filtering through the ice," said Rory. "And that creaking noise is the glacier moving very slowly between the two mountains." He seemed to know about everything.

They slid around a bend and skidded to a halt as they entered a vast ice cave.

"Wow!" said Abbi. "What a place!"

"It's a massive ice cave," said Rory. "And just look at all those long, thin icicles hanging from the roof. There must be thousands of them. Thousands and thousands."

The icicles glinted and shimmered with greens and blues, and gave the ice cave a ghostly light.

"And look at all the animals and Fur People," said Justin. "What a crowd."

A hum of noise went around the ice cave as everyone waited.

"There's Freeza," said Rory, and waved to the Fur Man.

Freeza waved back.

"But I can't see that big polar bear," said Abbi, "and I can't see Polar anywhere."

In the middle of the cave there was a platform made of ice, and on it stood a silver throne. Behind the throne there was a block of ice, and inside the block was something blue which throbbed and glowed, throbbed and glowed. It looked like a great stone.

"What a place," said Justin.

"It's fantastic," said Abbi.

"Amazing," said Rory.

The hum of noise grew louder as four grey wolves appeared from the far side of the ice cave.

Behind them were two people. One was an old Fur Man with a white beard. He carried a silver stick. The other was a tall woman. She wore a silver cloak and had a gold crown on her head.

They made their way to the ice platform in the middle of the cave. The tall woman took her place on the silver throne, and the old Fur Man with the white beard stood beside her. The hum of noise in the ice cave grew louder and louder.

"Silence!" shouted the Fur Man with the white beard. He banged on the ice platform with his silver stick.

"The Winter Queen," he said, and bowed towards the tall lady on her silver throne.

"The Winter Queen!" shouted the Fur People. "The Winter Queen!"

The shouts echoed round and round the ice cave. Rory looked up and saw how the echoes made the thousands of icicles shake. The Fur Man with the white beard banged his silver stick again, and the Fur People became silent.

The Winter Queen spoke. "Fur People and animals of WinterWorld," she said in a deep voice. "Thank you for coming to the Gathering. I have some bad news for you."

The crowd in the ice cave groaned.

"WinterWorld is in terrible danger," said the Winter Queen. "Our spies tell us that the HotSpotters are coming. They have declared war on WinterWorld."

A loud cry went up from the crowd. It echoed round and round the ice cave.

The old Fur Man banged his silver stick. "Silence!" he called.

"The HotSpotters are coming from VolcanoLand," went on the Winter Queen. "Once again they have sworn to destroy WinterWorld. They are terrorists who hate our peaceful way of life. They hate animals. They hate Fur People. They want to destroy the Blue Stone and to destroy WinterWorld."

The crowd groaned.

"All we want to do is live in peace and freedom," said the Winter Queen. "Will we let the HotSpotters destroy the Blue Stone?"

"No!" shouted the crowd.

"Will we let them destroy WinterWorld?"

"No! No!" shouted the crowd.

The shouts echoed round and round the ice cave, and once more Rory looked up and saw the icicles shaking.

"Look, Justin," he said. "Look at the icicles."

The boys watched as one icicle shook so much that it fell from the roof of the cave. It fell at high speed and hit the ice floor, just missing an Arctic fox. The fox jumped in fright as the icicle smashed into tiny pieces.

The old Fur Man banged his silver stick on the ice platform.

"Fur People and animals of WinterWorld," he said, "get ready to defend WinterWorld. We've beaten the HotSpotters before, and we will again. We will win!"

All the Fur People and animals began dashing here and there in the ice cave. It was time to protect WinterWorld against the evil HotSpotters.

Chapter 5
The HotSpotters

The animals hacked out blocks of ice from the cave walls with their hooves and antlers. Then the Fur People carried the blocks over to the ice platform and began to build a wall round it.

Justin, Abbi and Rory helped with the work, and block by block the ice wall grew higher.

After a lot of hard work the ice wall was finished. All the Fur People crowded round the ice platform inside the wall.

"Well done, everyone," said the Winter Queen. "You have built a wonderful ice wall. Will the HotSpotters be able to break it down?"

"Never!" shouted the crowd.

Justin was still worried. "Freeza," he said, "are we really safe behind this ice wall? Will it really keep out the HotSpotters?"

"It always has in the past," Freeza told him.

"And what is this Blue Stone thing?" asked Rory. "Why is it so important to WinterWorld?"

"It's an atomic stone," said Freeza. "It's the only one of its kind, and it controls the temperature. It keeps WinterWorld icy cold. Without it, WinterWorld would heat up and all our ice and snow would melt. Our world would end."

Justin and Rory looked at the Blue Stone. They watched it throb and glow, throb and glow in its block of ice behind the silver throne. But Abbi didn't care about the Blue Stone. She was busy looking for Polar, but there was no sign of him in the crush of Fur People and animals inside the ice wall circle.

Everyone waited for the HotSpotters to arrive. The hum of noise in the ice cave stopped. The silence was only broken by the creaking of the glacier as it slowly moved. High above their heads the thousands of icicles glinted with greens and blues.

Suddenly a Fur Man came racing down the ice passage and burst into the cave.

"The HotSpotters are coming!" he shouted.

A gasp of fear went up from the crowd of Fur People and animals inside the ice circle.

"There are more than a hundred of them," said the Fur Man as he was pulled to safety over the ice wall. "They'll be here in a minute," he gasped. "They were right behind me in the passage."

A cry went up from the WinterWorlders. It echoed round and round the ice cave. The icicles shook.

Two minutes later the first HotSpotter came stumbling into the cave. He skidded to a stop. Abbi's mouth fell open in surprise when she saw him.

The HotSpotter was tall. He was dressed in metal that glowed with heat. Big metal boots and gloves made his feet and hands look huge. He wore a huge metal helmet with six sharp spikes. But it was the HotSpotter's face that made Abbi tremble. It was red-hot, and he looked very, very angry. A twist of smoke came from his red ears. Steam rose from the cave floor where his hot boots were melting the ice.

"Hah!" shouted the HotSpotter when he saw all the Fur People and animals crowded inside the ice wall circle. "Hah!" he roared. His voice sounded harsh and cruel.

A second HotSpotter arrived, and then a third. More and more burst into the ice cave. They stood together, heat waves rising from their hot metal bodies. They pointed at the ice wall, and laughed loudly.

"This is it," Freeza said to the children. "This is war."

"But they haven't got any weapons," said Rory. "No swords, no guns, nothing."

"That's the only good thing about them," said Freeza. "They're not clever enough to make weapons. They just use their horrible hands and try to tear down our ice wall. But they always fail."

"How come?" asked Justin. "They should be able to pull apart an ice wall with those huge metal gloves. How come they always fail?"

"Wait and see," said Freeza. "Wait and see."

Now the tallest of the HotSpotters stepped forward. "WinterWorlders!" he shouted, and blasts of smoke shot from his ears. "I'm Hot-Shot, and I'm the leader of the HotSpotters. We're here to finish off WinterWorld once and for all. Right, lads?"

"Yes!" roared the HotSpotters.

"This time you WinterWorlders will be beaten," roared Hot-Shot. "This time WinterWorld will die!"

"Die!" roared the HotSpotters, and they shook their metal-gloved fists.

"Die! Die! Die! Die!" they roared.

Chapter 6
War!

"What can we do, Freeza?" asked Abbi, in fear. Freeza didn't answer. He broke off a small piece of ice from the wall and held it in his fur-gloved hand.

"Freeza," said Justin, "there's no way we can beat these – these terrorists."

"Oh, yes there is," said Freeza. "Just watch this!"

Freeza threw the small piece of ice at the leader of the HotSpotters. It hit Hot-Shot in the middle of his metal chest. At once, the ice melted with a hiss. Steam rose.

"Yeee-ah!" roared Hot-Shot, and wiped a big, metal glove across his chest.

"He didn't like that," said Rory.

"That's because he hates water," said Freeza. "It's the one thing HotSpotters can't stand. Water puts out their fire. It's how we beat them every time."

Freeza broke off another piece of ice and threw it at the HotSpotters. All the Fur People joined in. Soon lots of ice lumps went flying through the cave's chilling air and hit the HotSpotters.

The terrorists jumped and hopped as the ice melted on their red-hot bodies and helmets. They roared with anger as steam hissed.

"Yes!" shouted the WinterWorlders. "Yes!"

The hundred HotSpotters fell back. They stood at the side of the ice cave, steaming. They looked very angry indeed.

"Charge!" roared Hot-Shot.

The HotSpotters rushed forward, but were hit again and again as the WinterWorlders threw more and more ice lumps. Once more the HotSpotters fell back. Once more steam hissed from their red-hot bodies and spiked helmets.

"They're beaten!" shouted Freeza.

"Yes!" shouted the WinterWorlders.

"They'll soon be on their way back to VolcanoLand," said Freeza.

"Yes!" shouted the WinterWorlders.

Justin wasn't so sure. He was about to speak to Freeza when the leader of the HotSpotters began shouting.

"WinterWorlders!" he roared. "Don't think you've won, because you haven't. We have a secret weapon. We will beat you, you'll see. We will take prisoners back to VolcanoLand. We will destroy the Blue Stone, and finish WinterWorld forever!"

"Forever!" roared the HotSpotters.

"WinterWorlders!" roared Hot-Shot. "Do you give up now? Do you surrender?"

"Never!" shouted the WinterWorlders. "Never!" And they threw more ice lumps.

Hot-Shot steamed and smoked with red-hot anger. He waved, and a HotSpotter who'd been hiding at the back stepped forward. In his big, metal-gloved hands he held a long gun. He stood next to Hot-Shot, aimed the gun, and fired.

There was a loud whoosh! A long flame shot out and hit the ice wall. Blocks of ice melted at once.

The Fur People, the animals, the Winter Queen, Justin, Abbi and Rory were stunned. They stared at the hole in their ice wall.

Freeza could hardly speak. "They've – they've got – a weapon."

"It's a flame thrower," said Rory. "And it's a powerful one. Ice can't stand against that sort of heat. The ice wall will melt."

"But they've never had a weapon like that before," said Freeza.

"Well, they have now," said Justin, "and they're going to use it."

"Fire!!" roared Hot-Shot.

The flame thrower gun was fired again and again. It melted huge holes in the ice wall, and all the WinterWorlders drew back in fear. A few Fur People carried on throwing ice lumps but they were useless against the power of the flame thrower. Soon the ice wall circle was no more. It had just melted away.

The hundred HotSpotters rushed forward and made a ring around the frightened Fur People and animals. Now the WinterWorlders were at the mercy of the red-hot terrorists from VolcanoLand.

There was no way of escape. The WinterWorlders cried and groaned and whimpered.

"Quiet!" roared Hot-Shot. "Stand still!" The tall terrorist grunted, and gave a cruel laugh.

"I told you we'd win!" he roared. He shook his fist at the WinterWorlders. "You're beaten. We've won!" he roared.

"Hah!" roared the HotSpotters. "Winners!"

And they all did the high fives with their metal-gloved hands. "Winners! Winners!"

Their roars echoed round and round the ice cave. Yet again Rory saw how the thousands of icicles shook, and watched as one fell and smashed on the ice floor.

All the Fur People and animals were forced to sit down.

"Now," roared Hot-Shot, "we're going to choose some prisoners who'll be taken back to VolcanoLand."

Freeza, ten other Fur People, Justin, Abbi and Rory were picked out, and were lined up at the side of the ice cave.

"And old Whitebeard!" roared Hot-Shot.

Three HotSpotters dragged the old Fur Man off the ice platform. They broke his silver stick.

"And the Winter Queen!" roared Hot-Shot.

The HotSpotters dragged her off the silver throne and forced her to line up with the other prisoners.

Then a HotSpotter kicked the throne off the ice platform.

"Hah!" roared the HotSpotters. "Hah!"

Chapter 7
Now What?

Justin, Abbi and Rory stood in line with Freeza, the Winter Queen and the rest of the Fur People prisoners.

"Now what?" asked Justin. He looked more worried than ever.

"I'm afraid we've had it," said a very sad Freeza. "WinterWorld's finished, and *we're* going to be taken to VolcanoLand as prisoners."

Abbi was sobbing.

"But where is VolcanoLand?" asked Rory.

"Over the mountains," said Freeza. "It's a long, long way off. It's a place of fire. We'll never leave there alive."

But there was still work to be done by the HotSpotters before they left for VolcanoLand.

"Now for the Blue Stone!" roared Hot-Shot.

The HotSpotter with the flame thrower gun jumped onto the ice platform. He took aim at the Blue Stone that throbbed and glowed in its block of ice.

"Destroy it!" roared Hot-Shot. "Destroy the Blue Stone, and finish WinterWorld – forever!"

The hundred HotSpotters shook their big fists and roared. The WinterWorlders were silent with despair.

The HotSpotters roared and roared. They had won.

Rory looked up as the roars echoed round the ice cave. Again he saw the icicles shake, and one fell. It landed on top of a HotSpotter's helmet and melted.

"Yeee-ah!" cried the HotSpotter as steam rose from his head.

"Fire!" ordered Hot-Shot.

The gun shot a long flame and it hit the ice block. There was a loud hissing noise.

"Again!" ordered Hot-Shot. There was more steam and hissing when the flame hit the ice block.

The WinterWorlders groaned in despair.

But all was not lost. Not yet. The ice was so thick and hard that the block was still standing. The flames hadn't got through to the Blue Stone.

"Fire! Fire! Fire!" ordered Hot-Shot, and he began jumping up and down with anger.

The ice block was melting very, very slowly.

While this was going on Justin found time to wonder if he, Abbi and Rory would ever see High Farm again. He shuddered to think what might happen to them beyond the mountains in VolcanoLand. He could see all too clearly that these terrorists had no feelings for the lives of others – people or animals.

If only, thought Justin, *if only Polar and Abbi hadn't run onto the moor. If only ...*

"Fire! Fire! Fire!" roared Hot-Shot. Smoke poured from his ears, but still the gun's flames failed to get through to the Blue Stone.

Rory, like Justin, was lost in thought. *If only*, he thought, *he could find a way of getting out of this mess. If only he could find a way to beat the HotSpotters.* He raised his eyes to the ice cave's roof – and an idea flashed into his brain. Rory nudged Justin.

"What?" asked Justin.

"I've got an idea," said Rory, "to save WinterWorld."

Justin stared at Rory. Had he gone mad? Had the stress finally got to him?

Rory stepped from the line of prisoners. "WinterWorlders!" he called. "Listen to me!"

All eyes looked at the boy. Rory settled his glasses down onto his nose and said, "I want you to shout. All of you. Shout as loudly as you can!"

There wasn't a sound. The Winter Queen, Fur People, animals, Justin, Abbi, Hot-Shot and all the HotSpotters stared at the boy.

Yes, thought Justin, *Rory has gone mad. Completely mad.*

"Ready?" called Rory. "Everyone shout ... YES!"

There was nothing but a surprised silence.

Rory's voice cracked as he felt a prickle of panic, but he tried once more.

"Shout! Shout, YES!" called Rory, and he punched the chilling air with his fists.

One Fur Woman shouted, "Yes!"

Then a Fur Man and two Fur Children joined in. "Yes!"

"Louder!" called Rory. "Louder! LOUDER!" Suddenly all the Fur People, the prisoners in their line, Justin and Abbi shouted, "YES!"

Now the animals added their grunts, barks, growls and yelps.

"Stop it!" roared Hot-Shot. "Stop it now!" But no-one listened to him. Now all the Fur People and animals were on their feet.

"YESSSSSSSS!" they shouted. "YESSSSSSSS!"

The echoes raced round and round and round the ice cave. They bounced from one side to the other. The icicles started to shake. Everyone looked up and saw the thousands and thousands of green and blue icicles shaking and shaking. They saw one icicle fall and then another and another.

"It's raining icicles!" shouted Abbi in excitement. "It's raining icicles!"

Chapter 8
Who Won the War?

Everyone had to duck as thousands and thousands of icicles fell from the ice cave's roof. The pointed icicles stung the Fur People and animals, but they did far more harm to the HotSpotters.

Every terrorist from VolcanoLand was hit by at least a hundred icicles, and each icicle melted as soon as it touched the HotSpotters. Their metal helmets, boots,

gloves and bodies hissed and steamed. In seconds, the terrorists were soaked. Even the flame-throwing gun was wet through and useless.

"Yeee-ah!" cried the HotSpotters.

They jumped this way and that but they couldn't dodge the falling icicles.

"Stay where you are!" shouted Hot-Shot to the HotSpotters.

"We can't," they cried. "We're soaking. Our fires are going out!"

A huge icicle landed right on top of Hot-Shot's helmet. Water ran down the leader's angry, red face. Clouds of smoke shot from his ears.

"Let's get out of here!" he roared. "Before we die!"

The HotSpotters dashed out of the ice cave. They left their flame thrower gun behind on the ice platform. They charged away down the ice passage and out from under the glacier. They raced across the mountains and back towards VolcanoLand. But some of them didn't make it. Their fires went out – and they died in the snowy wastes of WinterWorld.

Back in the cave the last icicle fell from the roof. It smashed beside Justin without harming him.

One by one, the Fur People and the animals got to their feet. Someone lifted the silver throne back onto the ice platform. Others led the Winter Queen back to her place, and the old Fur Man with the white beard stood next to her. All the Fur People and animals gathered around.

"WinterWorlders," said the Winter Queen. "The HotSpotter terrorists have gone."

The crowd cheered.

"Once again, they have failed to destroy WinterWorld. Even with their terrible new weapon they have failed to destroy our priceless Blue Stone. WinterWorld lives on!"

Again, the crowd cheered.

Echoes bounced round the ice cave, but this time there were no icicles left to fall.

"The WinterWorld War is over," said the Winter Queen. "And we must thank the boy from WarmWorld for saving us."

All heads turned and all eyes looked at Rory.

Justin punched him on the shoulder, Abbi gave him a hug, and Freeza shook his hand.

Everyone crowded round and wanted to shake Rory's hand. He gave a shy smile.

While this was going on, Justin took Freeza to one side. "Freeza," he said, "we've got to get back home. Can you help us?"

"It's the least I can do," said Freeza, "After everything you have done for us."

Justin, Rory and Abbi waved goodbye to the WinterWorlders.

"Come back and see us sometime," said the Winter Queen. "You'll always be welcome in WinterWorld."

Justin, Abbi and Rory were just about to leave the ice cave when something furry and white came bounding up to Abbi.

"Polar!" shouted Abbi. "Polar, you're back!" She picked up her puppy and gave it a big hug. The puppy licked her face and wagged its little tail.

"That's it, then," said Justin. "Now we really *can* go home." And at last, at long last, the worried look vanished from his face.

Freeza led the children back across the frozen lake to the snowfield beside the pine forest.

"You'll have to go back through the same black hole," the Fur Man told them.

"No problem," said Justin.

"Get ready," said Freeza.

Rory held onto Justin's coat, and Justin grabbed Abbi's coat. Abbi hugged Polar tightly.

"We're ready," said Justin.

Freeza stood back. He did something strange with his hands, and a cold wind blew up from nowhere. Snow started to fall. In moments it became a blizzard.

"Goodbye," called Freeza. "Remember, we may need your help again some day – if the HotSpotters ever return."

"Goodbye," called Justin, Abbi and Rory.

The blizzard grew stronger. The wind howled. The three children and Polar were hurled high into the darkening sky.

Clinging together they were swept up and away ...

Up and away.

Who is Barrington Stoke?

Barrington Stoke was a famous and much-loved story-teller. He travelled from village to village carrying a lantern to light his way. He arrived as it grew dark and when the young boys and girls of the village saw the glow of his lantern, they hurried to the central meeting place. They were full of excitement and expectation, for his stories were always wonderful.

Then Barrington Stoke set down his lantern. In the flickering light the listeners were enthralled by his tales of adventure, horror and mystery. He knew exactly what they liked best and he loved telling a good story. And another. And then another. When the lantern burned low and dawn was nearly breaking, he slipped away. He was gone by morning, only to appear the next day in some other village to tell the next story.

Barrington Stoke would like to thank all its readers for commenting on the manuscript before publication and in particular:

Tim Abbey
Dennis Allen
Ross Allen
Neil Andrews
Charlotte Anthony
Nia Asensio
Sophie Baverstock
Elizabeth Bodkin
Anthony Brittain
Craig Bull
Ben Cheeseman
Rachelle Cope
Billy Paul Cox
Dr Michael R Davis
Charlotte Downey
Rebecca Downey
Yasmin Eresh
Chloe Georgeson
Mrs Gripper
Greg Harvey
Mrs Dawn Hunt
Dennis Jones
Kelly Marriott

Karen Elizabeth McIntyre
Fiona Mitchelson
Stehpanie Mullin
Luke Muncey
Leigh Anne Muncey
Sam Mussell
Karen Noble
Michaela North
George Ojjerro
Aaron Pardon
Stacey Price
Will Richardson
Ronnie Tony Shearing
Robert Stratton
Calum Trivass
Aiden Stanly Robert Trumble
Marc Wakeham
Dionne Ward
Alice Warner
Anna Warner
Sue Warner
Daniella Watson
Paul Young

Become a Consultant!

Would you like to give us feedback on our titles before they are published? Contact us at the address or website below – we'd love to hear from you!

Barrington Stoke, 10 Belford Terrace, Edinburgh EH4 3DQ
Tel: 0131 315 4933 Fax: 0131 315 4934 E-mail: info@barringtonstoke.co.uk
Website: www.barringtonstoke.co.uk

If you loved this story, why don't you read . . .

Ship of Ghosts

by Nigel Hinton

Have you sometimes longed for excitement and adventure? Mick has wanted to go to sea ever since his Dad was a sailor. His dreams come true. But what he discovers on the Ship of Ghosts turn his dreams into a nightmare.

You can order this book directly from:
Macmillan Distribution Ltd, Brunel Road, Houndmills,
Basingstoke, Hampshire RG21 6XS
Tel: 01256 302699